Welcome to ALADDIN QUIX!

If you are looking for fast, fun-to-read stories with colorful characters, lots of kid-friendly humor, easy-to-follow action, entertaining story lines, and lively illustrations, then **ALADDIN QUIX** is for you!

But wait, there's more!

If you're also looking for stories with tables of contents; word lists; about-the-book questions; 64, 80, or 96 pages; short chapters; short paragraphs; and large fonts, then **ALADDIN QUIX** is *definitely* for you!

ALADDIN QUIX: The next step between ready to reads and longer, more challenging chapter books, for readers five to eight years old.

Read more ALADDIN QUIX books!

By Stephanie Calmenson

Our Principal Is a Frog!
Our Principal Is a Wolf!
Our Principal's in His Underwear!
Our Principal Breaks a Spell!

A Miss Mallard Mystery
By Robert Quackenbush

Dig to Disaster
Texas Trail to Calamity
Express Train to Trouble
Stairway to Doom
Bicycle to Treachery
Gondola to Danger
Surfboard to Peril
Taxi to Intrigue
Cable Car to Catastrophe
Dogsled to Dread
Stage Door to Terror

Little Goddess Girls
By Joan Holub and Suzanne Williams

Book 1: *Athena & the Magic Land*
Book 2: *Persephone & the Giant Flowers*
Book 3: *Aphrodite & the Gold Apple*

Mack Rhino, Private Eye

Book 1: *The Big Race Lace Case*

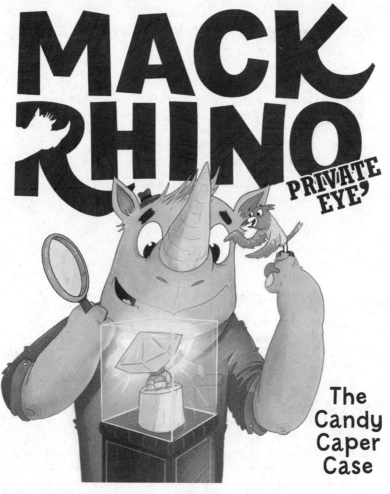

MACK RHINO

RHINO

'PRIVATE EYE'

The
Candy
Caper
Case

BY PAUL DUBOIS JACOBS AND JENNIFER SWENDER
ILLUSTRATED BY KARL WEST

ALADDIN QUIX

New York London Toronto Sydney New Delhi

For Nancy, always a sweetheart

ALADDIN QUIX
Simon & Schuster Children's Publishing Division
1230 Avenue of the Americas, New York, New York 10020
First Aladdin QUIX hardcover edition May 2020
Text copyright © 2020 by Jennifer Swender and Paul DuBois Jacobs
Illustrations copyright © 2020 by Karl West
Also available in an Aladdin QUIX paperback edition.
For information about special discounts for bulk purchases, please contact
Simon & Schuster Special Sales at 1-866-506-1949
or business@simonandschuster.com.
The Simon & Schuster Speakers Bureau can bring authors to your live event. For more information or to book an event contact the Simon & Schuster Speakers Bureau
at 1-866-248-3049 or visit our website at www.simonspeakers.com.
Book designed by Tiara Iandiorio
The illustrations for this book were rendered digitally.
The text of this book was set in Archer Medium.
Manufactured in the United States of America 0420 LAK
2 4 6 8 10 9 7 5 3 1
Library of Congress Control Number 2019955565
ISBN 978-1-5344-4116-3 (hc)
ISBN 978-1-5344-4115-6 (pbk)
ISBN 978-1-5344-4117-0 (eBook)

Cast of Characters

Mack Rhino, Private Eye: a detective

Redd Oxpeck: Mack's trusted assistant

Skunks McGee: a skunk who's up to no good

Shelly: director of the Beach Street Museum

Candy Cat: a new cat in town; a candy seller

A sweet lady: customer at the museum, bank, and jewelry shop

Terry Berry: Mack and Redd's friend; owner of Terry Berry's Smoothie Shack

Penny: new manager of the Beach Street Savings Bank

Queenie Zee: Mack and Redd's friend; owner of Queenie's Cupcakes

Gino: owner of Gino's Gems and Jewels

Contents

1

Spilled Milk

Snug in his office at Number 21 Beach Street, **Mack Rhino, Private Eye**, rolled up the blinds and rolled up his sleeves.

For cases big or small, Mack Rhino, Private Eye, was your guy.

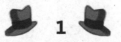

Or . . . rhino.

Mack poured himself a mug of chocolate milk. He took out his notebook. He reviewed his list.

Blinds ✓
Sleeves ✓
Chocolate milk ✓

Mack could now sit down to start his day.

Oops!

His rhino-size elbow bumped

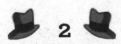 2

the cup. Chocolate milk spilled across the desk.

Mack quickly stood up.

Oops!

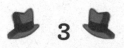

His other rhino-size elbow knocked over the carton. Chocolate milk spilled onto the floor.

Mack's trusted assistant, **Redd Oxpeck**, fluttered over with a dish towel. "You need more elbow room!" He giggled.

"Or smaller elbows," said Mack.

"Well, no use crying over spilled milk," said Redd.

Mack smiled. He wiped off his soggy notebook. He added this to his list:

Get more chocolate milk.

Say Cheese!

Despite the spill, Mack was in a fine mood. He and Redd had recently solved their one hundredth case.

Case #100—The Big Race Lace Case—had tied them up in knots.

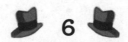

A lot was on the line . . . the finish line, that is. The Big Race was the biggest event of the year in Coral Cove.

The sneaky **Skunks McGee** had hired the Ant Hill Gang to take everyone's shoelaces. Luckily, Mack and Redd untangled the plot just in time.

But ever since, business had been quiet. Not a single call on the phone. Not a single knock at the door.

"So what's the plan for today,

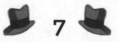

Boss?" Redd asked Mack.

"First stop," said Mack. "The corner store. We need more chocolate milk. After that, I'm not sure. Business has been . . ."

"Quiet?" said Redd.

"Exactly," said Mack.

"At least it's Friday," said Redd. **"Yahoo!** Bowling night! Plus, I have a surprise for you."

"A surprise?" asked Mack.

Redd held up a gleaming new camera. "Say cheese!"

Click! Flash!

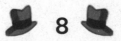 8

"I thought it would come in handy for our next case," said Redd.

"Good thinking," said Mack.

Mack and Redd looked down

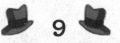

at the screen. Mack took out his magnifying glass. Only half of his face was in the picture.

"At least you got my good side," said Mack.

Ring-ring. Ring-ring.

That was a sound they hadn't heard in a while.

Mack picked up the phone. "Mack Rhino, Private Eye. For cases big or small, I'm your guy. Or . . . rhino."

But all Mack heard was a **high-pitched** noise.

Wee-oh! Wee-oh! Wee-oh!

It was so loud that Mack had to hold the phone away from his ear.

"Hello?" he shouted.

"Mack?" a voice yelled. "Is that you?"

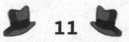 11

"Yes, it's me!" Mack shouted at the phone. "Who is this?"

"It's **Shelly** from the Beach Street Museum."

The Beach Street Museum was one of Coral Cove's most popular attractions. There was currently a special **exhibit** of rare and remarkable seashells.

"I have a mystery for you!" yelled Shelly.

"We'll be right there!" Mack shouted.

He hung up the phone. He tucked his notebook into his pocket.

"What is it, Boss?" asked Redd.

"I'm not sure," said Mack. "But it could be the start of Case #101!"

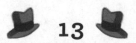

3

Shell Game

Mack and Redd hurried down Beach Street.

On the way, they passed a cat standing beside a fancy **pushcart**. In brightly painted letters, a sign read: **CANDY CAT**'S

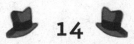

FAMOUS **CONFECTIONS**! IN TOWN
FOR ONE DAY ONLY!

A curious crowd had gathered
around.

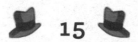

The cart held sweets of every stripe—hard candies, soft candies, sweet candies, sour candies, and chocolates in all shapes and sizes.

"Hey, Boss," said Redd. "Candy! Can we stop?"

"Maybe later," said Mack. **"Shelly needs us!"**

Mack and Redd hurried along. As they got close to the museum, the **piercing** noise got louder.

Wee-oh! Wee-oh! Wee-oh!

Mack and Redd rushed inside. Rare and remarkable seashells

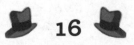 16

filled the **display** cases. Some were large. Some were small. Some were smooth, others spiky.

Wee-oh! Wee—

The noise went silent.

"Shelly?" Mack called. "Are you here?"

Shelly hurried out of the office. "I finally managed to turn off that burglar alarm," she said.

"Burglar alarm?" asked Redd.

"What was stolen?" asked Mack.

"That's the mystery," said Shelly. "*Nothing* was stolen. I don't

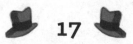

know why the alarm went off."

"Did you notice anything unusual?" asked Mack.

"No," said Shelly. "In fact, the museum has been quiet today . . . at least until the alarm went off."

"Even with the special exhibit?" asked Redd.

"Yes, the only visitors have been the two of you, plus **a sweet lady** who was here earlier," said Shelly.

"Can we take a look around?" asked Mack.

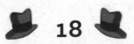

"Please do," said Shelly.

Mack and Redd inspected the museum.

Mack took out his magnifying glass. He jotted down notes in his notebook. Redd took photos with his new camera.

Everything seemed to be in order.

But Mack knew things weren't always what they seemed. Something just didn't feel right.

An empty museum?

A false alarm?

Mack needed to think. And Mack Rhino, Private Eye, did his best thinking sipping a Banana Supreme smoothie.

"Next stop . . . ," he said.

"Candy Cat's Famous Confections?" asked Redd hopefully.

"Soon," said Mack. "First, let's swing by **Terry Berry**'s Smoothie Shack."

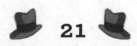

Bank Notes

Mack and Redd stepped up to the counter at Terry Berry's Smoothie Shack.

"What can I get you?" asked Terry.

"We'll have the usual," said Mack.

"Two Banana Supremes, coming right up!" said Terry. "One jumbo. One mini."

"Ready for bowling tonight, Terry?" asked Redd.

"You bet!" said Terry, handing Mack and Redd their drinks.

Mack looked around. Terry Berry's Smoothie Shack was usually buzzing with activity. Today, you could hear a pin drop.

"It sure is quiet," said Mack.

"Where is everybody?" asked Redd.

"I hear they're all at the new candy cart," said Terry. "Lucky for me, it's only in town for one day."

Just then someone tapped Mack on the shoulder.

"Excuse me," she said. "I'm looking for Mack Rhino."

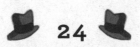

"That's me," said Mack. "And this is my trusted assistant, Redd Oxpeck."

"I'm **Penny**, the new manager at the Beach Street bank," she said. "I wonder if you can help me."

"What seems to be the problem?" asked Mack.

"Our alarm went **haywire** this morning," explained Penny. "And I don't know why."

"Is that so?" asked Mack.

"Another false alarm?" **chirped** Redd.

Mack and Redd finished their smoothies and followed Penny to the bank.

Again, they passed Candy Cat. Even more customers had lined up. He sure was doing a **brisk** business.

Mack, Redd, and Penny continued down Beach Street.

Number 12 was Queenie's Cupcakes. Number 11 was **Gino**'s Gems and Jewels. And Number 10 was the Beach Street Savings Bank.

Penny unlocked the front door.

"I've only had one customer today," she said. "The bank has been . . ."

"Quiet?" said Redd.

"**Precisely**," said Penny. "That is, until the alarm went off."

Mack and Redd inspected the bank. Mack jotted down notes in his notebook. Redd took photos with his camera.

Behind the counter, the dollar bills were wrapped and stacked. The coins were neatly organized

in their tray. Everything appeared
to be in order.

But what was that smell?

Mack sniffed the air.

It smelled **familiar**.

And . . . *delicious*.

Something didn't add up. Mack needed more information.

And nobody knew more about what happened on Beach Street than his good friend **Queenie Zee**, owner of Queenie's Cupcakes.

"Next stop . . . ," he said.

"Candy Cat?" asked Redd.

"Soon," said Mack. "First, let's go have a chat with Queenie."

 30

A Photo Finish

Mack and Redd walked down the street to Queenie's Cupcakes.

"I think I'll wait out here, Boss," said Redd. He held up his camera. "I'd like to snap a few outdoor shots."

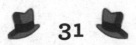

Mack nodded and went inside the shop.

"Hi, Mack," Queenie called.

"Hi, Queenie," said Mack. He looked around.

The popular Beach Street bakery was usually **humming** with customers. Today it was empty.

"Sure is quiet in here today," said Mack.

"It's the new cat in town," said Queenie. "It seems everyone is sweet on his sweets."

 32

"But nothing beats a Queenie cupcake," said Mack.

Queenie smiled. "And you, my friend, are just in time." She held up a tray of freshly baked cupcakes.

The smell was familiar.

And ... *delicious*.

Chocolate!

It was the same smell from the bank.

But why on earth would a *bank* smell like chocolate?

Wee-oh! Wee-oh! Wee-oh!

A loud noise cut short Mack's thoughts.

"Another alarm?" he said.

"It sounds like it's coming from Gino's Gems and Jewels," said Queenie.

 34

Mack charged out of the cupcake shop. He nearly bumped
into a sweet lady making her way
down the sidewalk with a cane.

"Pardon me, ma'am," said Mack.

"That's quite all right, dearie,"
said the lady.

Mack tipped
his hat.

"C'mon, Redd," he called. Then he and Redd rushed into Gino's.

Wee-oh! Wee-oh! Wee-oh!

"Hello?" Mack shouted over the loud noise.

"Just a minute," called Gino. "I need to turn off this alarm."

Wee-oh! Wee—

Gino appeared from the back room.

"Mack Rhino and Redd Oxpeck? What are you two doing here?" he asked, puzzled. "And what

 36

happened to my customer?"

"Customer?" asked Mack.

"The only customer I've had all day," said Gino. "Things have been . . ."

"Quiet?" said Redd.

"Exactly," said Gino. "Until the burglar alarm went off."

"Is anything missing?" asked Mack.

The display cases were filled with sparkling rings in a rainbow of colors. There were dazzling bracelets and necklaces, too.

 37

Gino examined the cases and said, "No, nothing is missing. I guess it's a false alarm."

Redd looked at Mack. "Three

false alarms in one day, Boss? What are the chances?"

Mack took out his notebook. He reviewed his notes.

> *Quiet museum.*
> *Quiet bank.*
> *Quiet store.*
> *Three loud alarms.*

Mack thought for a moment.

"Hey, Redd," he said. "Can we take a look at your photos? Maybe we missed something."

Redd **scrolled** through the

photos on the screen. Mack took out his magnifying glass to look.

There were pictures from the sidewalk outside Queenie's.

There were pictures from the bank.

There were pictures from the museum.

"Wait a minute!" said Redd, pointing. "This seashell looks a bit odd."

"Can you zoom in closer?" asked Mack.

Redd pressed a button.

The seashell closest to the bright display light was **misshapen**.

"Is that shell … *melting*?" asked Redd.

A *melting* shell? A bank that smelled like *chocolate*?

Mack suddenly had a hunch!

"Gino," he said, "could I try on one of your rings?"

"But of course," said Gino.

"Is now really the time for shopping, Boss?" asked Redd.

Mack picked up a ring with a gleaming red stone.

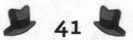

"That's one of my most expensive pieces," said Gino. "*You*, Mack Rhino, have excellent taste."

"And so does this ring," said Mack. He took a big lick. "Just as I suspected. Cherry!"

"I'm very confused," said Gino.

"Oh, I get it, Boss," chirped Redd. He picked up a bracelet. He took a big bite. **"Delicious!"**

Gino gasped.

"We'll explain in a minute," said Mack. "For now, follow us."

Partners in Crime

Mack, Redd, and Gino hurried out of the jewelry shop and over to the bank.

Penny was surprised to see them. She was even more surprised when Mack unwrapped a

stack of dollar bills and started nibbling.

"Just as I suspected," said Mack. "Milk chocolate! That's why the bank smelled familiar."

"Chocolate?" said Penny.

Redd unwrapped a coin. **"Yummy!"** he said. "These are *mint* chocolate."

"I'm very confused," said Penny.

"We'll explain soon," said Mack. **"Follow us!"**

They all hurried to the museum. Shelly was surprised to see them. She was even more surprised when Mack popped a rare shell into his mouth.

"Just as I suspected," he said. **"White chocolate!"**

"And this one is sea salt cara-mel!" added Redd.

"I'm very confused," said Shelly.

"Well, we've finally licked this case," said Redd, licking his lips . . . or beak.

"You have?" asked Shelly.

"Yes," said Mack. "Someone with sticky fingers has been steal-ing **valuables** and **replacing** them with candy copies!"

"*Candy* copies?" said Shelly.

"But who would have that much candy?" asked Penny.

 46

"You'd need a cart to carry it all," said Gino.

"Exactly!" said Mack. *"Candy Cat's Famous Confections!* Something tells me he's not as sweet as he appears."

"Except . . . ," said Redd.

"Except what?" asked Mack.

"Except Candy Cat has been out there selling candy all day," said Redd. "How could he be in *two* places at once?"

Redd was right. They had been up and down Beach Street. And

 47

each time they passed, Candy Cat was busy with customers.

Could Mack have it all wrong?

He took out his notebook. He reviewed his notes.

Then, suddenly, the whole picture came into focus.

Candy Cat *couldn't* be in two places at once.

"Didn't you each have a customer when the alarm went off?" asked Mack. "I'll bet Candy Cat has a partner in crime!"

"Oh, it couldn't have been my

customer helping Candy Cat," said Shelly. "She was a very sweet lady."

"My customer was a sweet lady, too," said Penny. "She did ask a lot of questions though."

"That sounds just like my customer," said Gino. "In fact, I had to leave her alone to look for the answers in my office."

"Me too!" said Penny and Shelly, both at the same time.

"Is that so?" said Mack. "Could you describe her?"

"Well, she had puffy white hair," said Shelly.

"She carried a large handbag," said Penny.

"She walked with a cane," added Gino.

"Hang on," said Redd, quickly scrolling through his photos. He held up his camera. "Is this her?"

It was a photo of the lady Mack had nearly bumped into on the sidewalk.

She had white hair.

She had a large handbag.

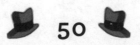

She had a red and white striped
cane.

"That's her!" they all said
at once.

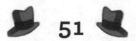

Redd zoomed in. "And that's not just any cane, Boss," he said.

Mack nodded. **"It's a candy cane!"**

Alley Oops!

Mack and Redd rushed outside. They looked up Beach Street. They looked down Beach Street.

But for the first time that day, Candy Cat was nowhere to be seen.

"Where did he go?" asked Mack.

"Time for a bird's eye view," said Redd. He fluttered high in the air.

"I see them!" Redd cried. "They're in the alley next to the corner store!"

Mack bounded over. Redd followed.

Hidden in the alley, Candy Cat was busy packing up his cart.

And he wasn't alone. The sweet lady from the photo was there as well. She clutched a **bulging** handbag.

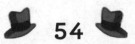

"Leaving so soon?" asked Mack, stepping into the alley. Redd fluttered over and perched on the cart.

"Sorry, we're closed," said Candy Cat.

"We're in a bit of a rush, dearie," said the lady.

"Then I'll get right to the point," said Mack. "I'm Mack Rhino, Private Eye, and I've had my eye on you."

The lady's sweet **expression** suddenly turned into a sourpuss.

 56

"Come on, Candy Cat," she said. "Leave the cart behind. Let's beat it!"

She tossed her cane to the side.

And the cat burglars took off **sprinting** down the alley.

"They're getting away, Boss!" cried Redd.

Mack stepped over to the candy cart. "Hmm, what should I try first?"

"Is now really the time for sweets, Boss?" asked Redd.

Mack grabbed a handful of jumbo gumballs.

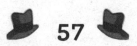

He took aim down the alley. He swung his arm back smoothly. He followed through.

And he bowled a perfect strike.

Candy Cat went splat.

The sweet lady tumbled.

Her handbag went flying.

"Hey, look what the cat let out of the bag!" said Redd.

Scattered on the ground were the real seashells, real dollar bills, real coins, and real jewelry.

Mack picked up a ring with a gleaming red stone. He gave it a big lick.

"Yuck." He smiled. "*Not* cherry."

"It was almost a perfect plan," said Redd. "Who would ever suspect a sweet old lady?"

He flew over and pecked at the strands of her puffy white hair.

"Just as I thought! Cotton candy!"

"And we *almost* got away with the goods," Candy Cat hissed.

"But you didn't," said Mack. "Because I'm Mack Rhino, Private Eye. For cases sweet or sticky, I'm your guy. Or . . . rhino."

Redd snapped one final photo.

Sweet Success

The team gathered at the Coral Cove Bowling Alley for bowling night.

Everyone wore their lucky striped bowling shirts and matching shoes.

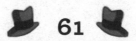

Mack brought the bowling balls for himself and Redd. One jumbo. One mini.

Queenie brought chocolate cupcakes. Terry brought Banana Supremes.

Redd arrived with a paper bag from the corner store.

"This is for you," he said to Mack.

Mack reached into the bag. **"Chocolate milk!"**

Mack took out his notebook. He added one final check.

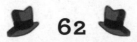

Get more chocolate milk. √

"And take a look at this, Boss," said Redd. He held up the *Beach Street Gazette* evening edition. "They printed my photo!"

Redd's photo appeared with the headline: "Candy Cat Burglars **Foiled**!"

"I guess you could say they were caught 'Redd-handed,'" said Queenie.

Mack Rhino, Private Eye, smiled. He could finally wrap up Case #101—The Candy Caper Case.

"There's just one thing," said Terry. "Whatever happened to all the candy?"

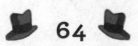 64

Word List

brisk (BRISK): Busy and active

bulging (BUL·jing): Bursting or swollen

chirped (CHERPT): Said excitedly

confections (kun·FECK·shuns): Fancy candies or sweets

display (di·SPLAY): A setup that is eye-catching for the viewer

exhibit (egg·ZIH·bit): A show or presentation, often in a museum

expression (ex·PRESH·un): The

look on someone's face showing emotion

familiar (fuh•MILL•yer): Well known

foiled (FOY•uld): Stopped

haywire (HAY•why•er): Out of order or out of control

high-pitched (hi•PICHT): Screeching or shrill

humming (HUH•ming): Busy and lively

misshapen (miss•SHAPE•in): Not having the right shape; distorted

piercing (PEER•sing): Very loud and high-pitched

precisely (preh•SISE•lee): Exactly

pushcart (PUSH•kart): A cart moved by hand and used to sell things

replacing (ree•PLAY•sing): Taking the place of something else

scrolled (SKROLD): Flipped or moved through words or pictures

sprinting (SPRIN•ting): Running quickly

valuables (VAL•yoo•uh•bulls): Expensive things

 69

Questions

1. At the beginning of the story, Mack gets a strange phone call. Who is calling? What else does Mack hear?

2. Why are Terry Berry's Smoothie Shack and Queenie's Cupcake Shop so quiet today? Where are all the customers?

3. What do the museum, the bank, and the jewelry shop have in common? What happened in all three places?

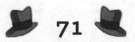

4. What does Mack notice about the seashell near the display light in Redd's photograph? How does this help him to solve the mystery?

5. Redd likes to take photos with his new camera. Do you like to take pictures? What kinds of things do you like to take pictures of?